DESERT KINGS

Veronica

Stranded with the Sheikh

By Jennifer Lewis

Published 2014 by Mangrove
2637 E Atlantic Blvd #24692
Pompano Beach, FL 33062
USA

ISBN 978-1-939941-12-1

1

All taut, tanned muscle and flashing blue eyes, Zadir Al Kilanjar was trouble. Ronnie Baxter could see that from a mile away. Right now she sat only a few feet away across the aisle of a private jet, flying from one business meeting in Dubai to another in Bahrain. For the first hour of the flight, she'd buried herself in a thriller, while he scrolled and typed on a sleek piece of technology.

"Veronica, right?" His deep voice penetrated the silence of the cabin.

She steeled herself to meet his gaze. "Yes." She didn't know him well enough to tell him that everyone called her Ronnie. He might think she liked him or something.

"Am I imagining things or did the engine just cut out?"

She tugged her earbuds out. She used them to block out the outside world more often than she cared to admit. The cabin hum sounded normal to her. She glanced out the window at the forbidding desert below. "We're still flying."

"I suppose we are." He flexed his arms, pulling his white T-shirt tight over a broad chest. It really wasn't right for a man to look that good when he stretched.

"I feel like we should be there by now."

She tugged her eyes from his hard, flat stomach. "It's difficult for me to judge. This is my first trip to the Arabian peninsula and everywhere seems to be thousands of miles apart with nothing but sand in between."

"Not on this flight." She noticed the slight dimple in his left cheek. Definitely trouble. Cute slightly British accent, too. "We're going from one part of the coast to the other."

She turned and frowned at the dunes below. "Then shouldn't we be near water?"

"Yes. If you see land it means we're coming down any minute."

A nasty feeling snuck over her and she put down her e-reader. "Look out the window."

He gave her a curious glance. He'd pulled down the blind on his side before takeoff and sat in the aisle seat. He probably traveled so often that he found the spectacular earth-from-space view routine. No doubt the region's perpetual sunshine was simply annoying screen glare. He leaned over, giving her an uncomfortably intimate view of his sculpted backside, jerked up the blind and peered out the oval porthole on the far side. "Holy shit."

He turned back quickly. "It looks like we're over the Rub' Al Khali. The Empty Quarter."

Another glance out her window confirmed the view of nothing but peaks and valleys of sand, blistering blue sky pressed down against them. The harsh sun cast shards of light off the plastic plane window. "What does that mean?"

"It means we're flying the wrong way. Bahrain is on the coast. Let me go talk to the pilot." He put his tablet on the seat next to him and rose. Her eyes followed his broad shoulders as he strode purposefully down the short aisle toward the cockpit.

She hadn't wanted to come here, but oil billionaires made good architecture clients, at least if you were ambitious and wanted to create something bold and powerful, not just another craftsman-style house on a suburban hill. Earlier today, she'd met with a brokerage owner in Dubai who wanted a landmark headquarters. Now she was on her way to attend the wedding of a man she'd met once, who wanted her to design a coastal retreat for him and his new bride in Bahrain. More money than God, apparently, so worth her time and effort.

Zadir struggled with the handle on the cockpit door. "It won't open." He banged with his fist.

Panic surged through her, and she rose to her feet. "Maybe he's dead? Or unconscious?" They weren't all that high above the dunes.

"Sit down and buckle in." Grim determination had replaced Zadir's flirtatious expression. He pulled his billfold out of his back pocket, used a credit card to trip the lock, then burst in. Within seconds he yelled out. "The pilot's gone. Get up here."

The shock of his brusque order stung for a split second before his words sank in.

The pilot's gone.

Heart pounding, she fumbled with her seat belt, then sprang to her feet. Where could he go? She hurried down the aisle and pushed into the bright cockpit, with its intimidating array of dials and levers.

"A window is missing. It's not broken, either. The frame's been unscrewed. It must have been deliberately removed." Zadir was scanning the equipment, peering at the lettering on the controls. She glanced about and saw one of the side windows completely gone.

"How come we're not being sucked out?"

"Low altitude. He wasn't sucked out either. He must have jumped some time after takeoff."

It was hard to believe. She searched the tiny cockpit for signs that he was there, hiding, waiting to spring out at them, but it was too small for even a cockroach to hide. The missing window scared her. She could feel a breeze and didn't want to go any closer. "Do you know how to steer it back?"

Zadir didn't turn from the dashboard. "We won't make it back. Or anywhere else, either. We're out of fuel." He pointed to the gauge, which was below the E for empty. "Right now we're gliding."

She gulped. "What do we do?"

"I tried to send a Mayday on the radio, but it's been disabled. He must have cut the wires."

"Why?" her voice came out a frightened whisper.

"I don't know, but we need to get this thing down safely before it loses momentum."

"Here in the desert?"

"We don't have a choice."

"Do you know how to land a plane?"

"I've taken a couple of lessons, and the controls are pretty standard."

A couple of lessons? The missing window gave a crystal-clear view of hot blue sky and hotter amber sands. Panic quickened her breath and made her hand spring to her mouth as if to stifle a scream.

Zadir grabbed her shoulder. "Keep your head. Sit down and buckle in. Assume the crash position." He was already buckling into the pilot's seat. "The good thing is that the sand should make for a fairly soft landing and there's no fuel to start a fire."

"Comforting." Her fingers trembled so much she had a hard time closing her buckle. "I hope the plane doesn't break up on landing."

"Me too."

Although he'd told her to put her head down, she couldn't take her eyes off the windshield as he guided the plane lower, and the dunes rose up toward them. A scream tickled the back of her throat while he struggled to keep their course straight and the ground rushed toward them.

"Brace!"

She pressed her head to her knees before a jarring, bumping, rolling motion seized the cabin as the plane sledded across the desert floor. They came to a complete standstill in seconds, not like the long taxiing at an airport. She lifted her head gingerly. "We're down?"

"Yup. And still alive." He smiled.

A wave of relief washed over her. She'd survived a plane crash thanks to this man. "Thank you."

"Don't thank me yet. We're probably hundreds of miles from anywhere. We need to find a way to get out of here."

He climbed out of his seat and headed back into the cabin. The plan had landed at an angle so he grabbed at the seats as he made his way down the aisle and pulled a phone from his bag. "I'm going to try to call for help, but I don't have high hopes since we are quite literally in the middle of nowhere."

She pulled out her phone and looked for bars. None.

"Service is patchy even in the main city of my

home country. We're still catching up with the twentieth century out here, let alone the twenty-first." He frowned, punching numbers into his phone. "Nothing."

"Surely someone would notice the plane going off its planned route."

"Except that this isn't a Boeing 747 going from London to Paris. It's a private corporate jet chartered by my friend Najib to carry us to his wedding."

"Hopefully Mr. Al Makar will notice when we don't show up."

"He'd better. I'm his best man." His blue eyes flashed grim humor. "But they won't think to look for us out here in the desert. We'll be lucky if anyone flies over at all."

The air in the plane was getting hotter. "Do you think we should try to get outside?" She could see sand almost up to the level of the windows on one side and had a sudden vision of suffocating in there.

"Yes, but first let's find out what we have for water and food. There should be water supplies on the plane for events such as this." They dug through the area in the back of the plane that served as a small galley and discovered that the two five-gallon jugs of water that should have been secured there had been removed.

Deep foreboding clawed at her gut. "I'm starting to get a feeling that someone wants us dead."

"Or wants me dead, and you have the bad luck to be with me." His chiseled features tightened. "My brother Osman has suspected some kind of conspiracy against our family since our father died." He looked right at her. "My father was king of a country you've probably never heard of."

"Ubar." She knew more about Zadir Al Kilanjar than she cared to admit, due to her weakness for celebrity gossip. "I read about his death in the paper, and that he divided the kingdom among his three sons."

He nodded. "Can't say I was too happy about it. In general, I prefer the Left Bank of Paris to the empty desert. Damn, there's no food, either." The mini-fridge was empty, not even an ice cube in the tiny freezer compartment.

"I have some water in my bag." She walked back to her seat, balancing herself on the seat backs. She had four small bottles of Evian and a big mister of spring water.

"What's the spray bottle for?" He joined her.

"My skin gets dry on airplanes." She felt a little embarrassed by it. "Spritzing it feels really good." She fished around the bottom of her bag and pulled out a bag of cashews and an energy bar. "But this is all the food I have."

"I'm glad you're a good traveler. I don't even have a single peanut or a drop of water."

"I'm happy to share." Then she felt stupid for saying it. What kind of person wouldn't share her water with someone after a plane crash in the desert? "Though I don't suppose it will last long."

They couldn't get the door open. Too much sand against it. In the end, she offered to squeeze out through the small window in the cockpit. It had been removed deliberately, all the rivets unscrewed.

She eased herself through headfirst, like a baby emerging from the birth canal, and the heat outside took her breath away.

"Careful, the sand is burning hot."

She wore little ankle boots, thank goodness, not her usual sandals, since she was traveling on business. A survey of the door showed only about a foot of sand piled against it, and she quickly kicked it away with her feet so Zadir could open the door from the inside. He filled the doorway as he emerged, squinting into the sun. "I think we should walk to the highest point and see if we can see anything at all. A city, an oil installation, a Bedouin caravan."

"The highest point is probably the top of that dune over there." It wasn't far, and it was a good hundred feet up in the air and looked like an intimidating climb. "Though I didn't see anything from the plane."

"Me either, but I was hyperfocused on landing. We'll go slow and conserve energy. No sense sweating out all our water." They headed out across the burning sands. Unfortunately, it was the thick, deep type of sand, like a beach, and made for slow going. They climbed laboriously to the razor-edged peak of the highest dune, sliding backward and clawing their way in the burning sand until they straddled the top and looked around at the breathtaking view of…

2

Absolutely nothing. Amber dunes stretched for miles in every direction. Hardly a big surprise but still a hope-sapping disappointment.

They stood in silence for a minute, maybe two or three. "I feel like my life should be flashing before my eyes," she said at last. "This isn't good."

His chest rose and fell as he let out a sigh. "I can't argue with you."

Sweat trickled down her back under her thin blouse. She could feel her already dark skin tanning in the sun. When she looked back toward the plane she was alarmed by how easily it blended in with the sun-glare-lit sand. "How would anyone even see us if they flew over?"

"We should do something to attract the eye. Do you have any bright clothes?"

She shook her head. "I usually wear black or white."

"I suppose I do, too."

She rubbed her mouth thoughtfully. "Maybe we should make a big shape, like a circle. A familiar outline that draws the eye and breaks up monotony. It's something we do in architecture all the time."

"You mean with our footprints."

"With anything we can find."

Zadir led the way as they trekked back to the plane. His T-shirt clung to his athletic muscles, and his damp hair accented his bold features. She cursed herself for noticing at a time like this. Maybe her brain was playing tricks on her. They could die out here and she was thinking about how hot he was?

Probably the human survival instinct. Hopefully, she'd prove civilized enough not to claw his clothes off in a desperate last-ditch attempt to continue the species.

He glanced back at her, then lifted a dark brow. "You're smiling."

"I think I'm going crazy."

"Have some water." They climbed back into the plane, where he offered her one of her own Evian bottles. "People are often found dead of thirst with water still in their canteens. Let's not go down like that."

She took a swig, surprised at how good it tasted. "We're going to survive this."

"Damn right we are." He took a gulp from another bottle. "And show those bastards they can't take down an Al Kilanjar."

"Who do you think it is?"

He shook his head. "Our country hasn't had a war with any of the neighbors in decades. Ubar's been a sleepy throwback to another era while the countries around us have exploited their oil and prospered. My brothers and I plan to bring Ubar up to speed and there are some traditionalists who are cranky about reforms we plan to make, but I don't think they're angry enough to kill us. Traditionalists usually still have respect for the ruling family."

"Perhaps it's someone with an economic interest." She wiped her lips with the back of her hand.

He stared at her for a moment. "Quite possibly. But that's the least of my worries right now. Let's go make a shape."

They laid out anything they could find in the plane that wasn't nailed down—magazines, toilet paper, pages from her notepad, seat cushions, curtains—and joined them together with a network of footprints, until they'd made the plane a target at the center of a circle about fifty feet across.

As they walked back to the plane she felt a weird sense of accomplishment, and a sudden breeze provided a rush of relief. Maybe they'd get out of this thing alive after all. "Damn, that wind feels good."

But when she turned to look at Zadir, he was frowning. "Wind can be a friend or an enemy."

"Why?"

"Sandstorms." As they climbed up through the door, the gusts started to toss around the objects they'd laboriously placed. Soon magazine pages fluttered and toilet paper took flight. Then the first grains of sand stung her arms and legs.

"Quick, get inside." Zadir helped her in and closed the door.

She looked out the window as sand blurred the view of more sand. "We're really screwed now, aren't we?"

"It's merely a setback." He rested his hand on her upper back, which provoked an instant physical response, tightening her nipples under her blouse and sending a shiver of awareness to her fingertips. She cursed her body and the mind she was obviously losing. He slid his hand lower, to her waist. "I have an idea."

"Oh?"

"Come this way."

3

He guided her along the tilting aisle. Inside the plane the air was cooler than outside, and the plush leather seats and expensive detailing of the private jet looked incongruously luxurious compared to their harsh surroundings.

"They may have taken all the food and water, but we have hundreds of towelettes." He picked up a sachet from a full box, ripped it open, and shook out the damp white cloth inside. "Refreshment awaits you."

She laughed. How could she not? "You're good at looking on the bright side."

"It's probably my fault that we've been stranded here so I'd be happy to atone by cooling your skin."

"I can do it myself, thanks." She took a handful of towelettes, still smiling.

He was already stripping off his T-shirt, and she averted her eyes from the arrogant display of tanned muscle that was his back. Did he expect her to undress too? She decided to wipe off her arms, where a fine layer of sand made her skin look ashy. The cool sensation of the wipe—which was probably loaded with alcohol and very drying—was wonderful on her sticky, hot skin.

"Good, right? Would you mind doing my back? I can't reach." He demonstrated that the thickness of his own biceps made it impossible for him to reach the middle of his back.

She gulped. "Okay." She opened a fresh towelette and drew it slowly down the hollow of his spine. Goodness. She had never done anything like this with a man she didn't know intimately. And her longest relationship had been with a boyfriend who was ticklish and didn't relish being touched unnecessarily.

When the towelette had absorbed the heat and salt from his skin, she unwrapped another one and started to wipe his right shoulder.

"What do you do, when you're not stranded in the desert?"

"I'm an architect."

"What kind of buildings do you design?" His muscles rippled slightly as he spoke. His body was beautifully proportioned, sturdy and masculine as a classical statue.

"Stark minimalism, I'm afraid." Which was lucky, or she'd be tempted to commission a statue of Zadir Al Kilanjar for her garden.

"Don't apologize. I'm a fan of minimalism myself. I almost bought a Kouichi Kimura house last year, but someone beat me to it."

"No kidding?" She rubbed another towelette over his left shoulder. "Kimura's houses are beautiful, but I mostly do larger buildings, offices, government buildings, that kind of thing."

"You prefer to work on a grand scale."

"I do. I try to take commissions that will still be there in a hundred years. Unless the money's too good to pass up, of course." She sighed. "That's why

I'm flying to Bahrain to meet with Mr. Al Makar."

"You're going to design Najib's house?"

"I haven't committed yet. If he's going to give me free rein with design and budget, I'll seriously consider it."

"He'll be a fantastic client. Though perhaps I shouldn't tell you that. I need a residence for myself, and I suspect you would be the perfect designer."

She paused in her stroking. "I really don't do many houses."

"This is more of a palace. As you already know, I inherited a third of my father's kingdom, and in his wisdom he saw fit to give me the emptiest, most desolate tract. There's not a single building on it, not even a shed."

"A blank canvas." She stroked again, trying to distract herself from thoughts of building a palace. Palaces lasted hundreds of years—if no one killed the monarch and destroyed it, of course.

"Yes, and you'd find me a very tractable client. I have no idea what I want except that it needs to fit the desert setting and have the smallest carbon footprint possible. You must give me your card."

She laughed. "You sound like I'm about to get off this plane and walk away."

His shoulders shook with laughter. "If only. What's your last name?"

"Baxter, Veronica Baxter. Please call me Ronnie."

"I'd love to pretend I've heard of you, but I'll plead ignorance."

"I'll admit your plea. I won an American Institute of Architects award last year."

"I'm impressed. And I need a palace."

"At least you hope you do. We have to get out of

here first." She stroked the back of his neck, disturbing the strands of dark hair there. They'd both cooled down enough to stop sweating, but her core temperate kept rising due to proximity to this breathtakingly handsome man—who'd saved her life.

He reached around and took hold of her wrist gently but firmly. "We're going to be fine. You do believe that, don't you, Ronnie?"

She drew in an unsteady breath. "I think so."

"They'll send out a search party." He still held her wrist. She thought that maybe she should try to tug it back, but she didn't. "We'll be drinking champagne by tomorrow afternoon, probably."

"Wouldn't that be nice?"

"Stay here." He rose, and again his brusque command made her raise a brow, but she took the opportunity to rub a cool cloth over her own neck and shoulders, under her blouse. Zadir retrieved their Evian bottles from the no doubt rapidly warming fridge and handed hers to her. She took a sip. "That tastes better than the most expensive champagne right now."

He grinned, revealing that cute dimple. "I guess adversity makes you appreciate the important things."

"Our plane would have landed by now."

"A long time ago. It's night." He gestured to the window, where darkness eclipsed the swirling sand. The cabin still had small lights on along the floor and ceiling. Probably battery powered. "I'm sure people are wondering where we are."

"I hope they are. Do you have a wife or girlfriend to worry about you?" She half hoped he did. That would make it easier for her to stop noticing every artistic curve of his physique.

"Nope." He took a swig of Evian. "It's times like this when I wish I did. Even my brothers won't wonder where I am. They're not expecting me back in Ubar for two days. How about you? Do you have someone to worry?"

She looked down at her bottle, then thumbed the smooth glass at the top. It was Friday night. "Except for your friend Najib, who's pretty busy with his wedding, no one will even notice I'm missing until I don't show up at my office on Monday. Even then, my assistant will probably assume I'm meeting with a client and forgot to tell her."

"You don't have any family?"

"Not really. No one that would miss me." She didn't remember ever feeling like she'd had a real family. She wouldn't know how to make one if she tried.

"Don't look sad. We're going to be fine. I find it hard to believe you don't have a husband or boyfriend."

She cocked her chin. "I'm married to my work."

"Oh." A mischievous smile snuck across his mouth. "I'm glad to hear that."

"Why?" She lifted a brow.

"I'd like the architect for my palace to be utterly devoted to the project, of course."

"I haven't said I'll design your palace."

"Indeed you haven't, but I can be very persuasive."

"You haven't even seen my work."

"I feel confident that it's stunning and memorable in every way." The way he said the words, slowly and softly, with a deft appraisal of her face and body, made her feel as if he was talking about her. Worse yet, she liked it.

Which was ridiculous. Men didn't exactly fall at her feet. She was tall and skinny and was the only black girl in the world who didn't have a butt. And she was cold and stuck-up, or at least that's what people said. She knew it was just shyness.

"You're sweet." She smiled. She was lucky to be stuck with someone nice, let alone gorgeous, out here in the desert.

"Sweet enough for you to let me soothe your skin with these luxurious wipes?"

Her skin heated further at the prospect of his big hands on her. "Okay."

4

Ronnie couldn't believe she was sitting in a private jet wearing only a bra on top. But the cool wipes were working magic, which Zadir made more intense by blowing softly on her damp skin.

It was as close to bliss as you could get when you were trapped in a desert wilderness in a crashed plane.

"Were you surprised when you suddenly inherited a kingdom?" She'd started to feel relaxed around him. "I read in a magazine that originally your oldest brother was supposed to inherit."

"It was a total shock and not a pleasant one. I wanted to give the kingdom back to my brother Osman. He convinced me that we could all work as a team to bring Ubar into the modern world."

"Is it backward there?"

He laughed. "We prefer the word *traditional.* But the truth is that lot of the population is illiterate, and lives much the same way they have for a thousand years. We're starting to tap into the natural resources so we can release a lot of wealth to improve life for the people and catch up with the other countries in the region."

"Your father wasn't interested in exploiting the oil?"

"He had plenty of money to fulfill his personal needs from the high taxes he imposed on everyone. He lived for pleasure and didn't worry too much about anything else."

"It doesn't sound like you really miss him."

Zadir's hands stilled on her back. "I don't miss him at all. I barely knew him. He had little time for children. And if the rumors are true, he had my mother killed when he grew tired of her."

"What?" She tensed, wanting to turn and see his expression but not wanting to intrude. She could hear emotion in his voice.

"Divorce is illegal in Ubar. If a man grows bored with his wife, he can cheat and be looked down on by his peers, or he has to somehow dispose of her." His voice had lowered to a growl.

"I hope you're planning to change that rule."

"It's at the top of the long list of things we intend to address. We have to proceed cautiously, or we'll have a revolution on our hands. Luckily my brother Osman is a natural diplomat, so he's good at knowing what to present and when. My brother Amahd is in charge of bringing the country's oil and gas resources to market. He's been in oil exploration for some time so he knows what he's doing." His hands now moved confidently over her back again. She shivered as he pressed a new, cool towel to a sensitive spot on the side of her waist.

"What's your role in the future of Ubar?"

He paused again. "To be determined. I'm a real estate investor. Not much use for that in a place where the only real estate is mud-brick houses people build with their bare hands. So far I've been focusing on education and how to bring regular schooling to the children. Right now we're leaning toward some kind of Internet solution."

"Education is important, but it sounds like you should also be creating infrastructure."

"You mean houses and buildings?"

"And roads. Surely you'll need all of them to support the oil development."

His fingertips rested right at her waist. She could almost hear his brain working. "You're right. The population is scattered. They don't live in tents so much any more, but little houses here and there in the hills. We'll need to bring in skilled labor from outside to train people as well."

"You'll need to build a town." Her skin prickled with possibilities that had nothing to do with the handsome man behind her. What architect didn't dream of creating a town from the ground up?

"I suppose you're right. And I suspect you could help me with that." His hands almost circled her waist. Her breathing had quickened, but she tried not to get too excited.

"You imagine correctly. In fact it would be a dream commission."

"As soon as we get out of here—and attend to our business in Bahrain—you must come visit Ubar and explore the possibilities."

"I'd love to." She shivered slightly as he pressed a new wipe against her neck. "I think I'm cool enough now. There's no need to keep stroking me with those things." With all the excitement there was a real danger she might explode into flames.

"The temperature's dropping. The desert can get quite cold at night."

"Right now that sounds good." As long as it didn't

get so cold that they had to huddle together for warmth. She wasn't sure she could stand much more proximity to Zadir. And now, with the enthralling possibility of creating a whole town hanging in the balance, she had every reason to keep their relationship professional.

Zadir rose. "I'm going to go tinker with the radio again. These cabin lights mean there's still some kind of power. And if I can find a way to turn on some emergency outside lights, I'll do that, too. We might be easier to spot in the dark than during the day with enough light."

"How long do you think these lights in the cabin will last?"

He shrugged. "We've had time to get the lay of the land, so we'll be fine until morning if they go out."

She watched him walk, shirtless and dangerously gorgeous, back across the tilted plane to the cockpit. She pulled a clean shirt from her bag and slipped into it. With everything in her carry-on, she was perfectly prepared to be stuck somewhere for a night, with water and snacks and a change of clothes. She changed her underwear and pants quickly, too, now that Zadir was occupied. She might as well feel fresh.

There was almost no chance they'd be rescued tonight. If a control tower was tracking their flight path and saw that they'd crashed, rescuers would have arrived there by now.

She checked her phone, but there were still no bars so she turned it off to conserve what was left of the battery life. How odd to be in the twenty-first century, in the middle of a continent ringed by cities, and be as completely cut off from civilization as if they were stranded on a desert island.

The grim thought propelled her from her chair and into the cockpit with Zadir. Usually she liked to be alone, but right now she needed human contact, maybe just to reassure herself that she wouldn't spend her last hours in this plane.

"Any luck?"

He was crouched on the floor, the pilot's headphones over his ears, broad back bent over something. "I'm trying to see if the pilot cut some wires that I can patch back together. A lot of this technology looks advanced from the outside but is pretty primitive once you peek under the dash. I've found one loose end, and if I can figure out where to connect it, we might be in business."

"What can I do to help?" She hated feeling useless.

He pushed the headset aside so one ear was exposed. "Talk to me. Your voice soothes me."

"You don't seem like you need soothing. You strike me as very calm."

He looked up, a wry smile on his face. "I'm doing my best to stay cool."

"It's working. What does get you rattled?"

"Losing out on a great deal." Then he frowned. "And any interaction with my father used to get me wound up. That's why I learned to avoid him. He shoved us off to boarding school abroad, then wanted us to pretend he was the greatest dad in the world on the rare occasions we saw him."

"I know that scenario." The confession surprised her, but it felt right.

"Your dad was like that, too?"

She swallowed. "Very much so. My parents got divorced when I was three and I saw him once a year at the most after that. He'd invite us over, then we'd be at a loose end while he played tennis or something. He felt that sending money to support us was enough to make him the father of the century."

"Is he still alive?"

"Alive and well and has the second-largest number of semiconductor patents in the USA. He's on his fifth or sixth wife. I've lost count. Luckily, he makes enough money to support all of them. I couldn't wait until I got old enough to support myself and get off the payroll."

Zadir crouched, still listening. "Your mother is still alive?"

"Yes. If you can call it that. She rarely leaves her Upper West Side apartment. In fact, she spends most of the day in bed popping prescription pills. She was a singing star for about twenty minutes around the time she met my dad, but she lost all interest in working once he began to pay for everything."

"So she probably wasn't the greatest parent in the world, either."

She grimaced. "Not by a long shot. Lucky for me, I had a good nanny for some of my formative years, and I learned to depend on my own resources at an early age."

"Damn, your childhood sounds almost as fun as mine. Did you go to boarding school?"

"Of course." She smiled ruefully. "Boarding school is the salvation of wealthy and neglectful parents. I went to Smithson Ladies Academy in Foxton, Connecticut, which was an ongoing contest for who had the most expensive designer toys. How about you?"

"Eton. Not so different but pretty fun all the same."

"Were you there with Prince Harry?"

He nodded, blue eyes sparkling. "And he's every bit as wild as the newspaper stories would have you believe."

"I suspect you are, too." She said it with a joking tone, half hoping he'd contradict her. His reputation as a ladies man might be just a rumor.

"Probably." His mischievous grin confirmed her worst fears. "But now that I'm a monarch with a reputation to protect I've turned over a new leaf. I'm sober as a judge and twice as dull." He rose from the floor and sat in the pilot's chair.

"I find that hard to believe." Especially since he was flirting with her right now. She wasn't going to fall under his spell like all those other silly girls. "You must have more women after you than ever now you're going to be a king."

"The funny part is that I have to marry one in order to take the throne. It was one of the conditions of my father's will."

"Why would he do that?"

"To make us all settle down, I suppose. But he seems more than a little hypocritical, considering how he treated the institution of marriage. I'm sure he thought his wives were the ones with the problems. To tell you the truth, my father's behavior has always scared me off marriage."

"You're afraid you'll grow bored and want out?"

"Who isn't? Forever is a very long time."

"You'll feel differently when you fall in love. At least that's what everyone says."

"But you don't believe it." He leaned back in the chair.

"I don't intend to place my happiness in anyone

else's hands." She sat in the copilot's seat. "I'm quite happy with my work."

"Your buildings are your children." He looked curious.

"I suppose they are, yes."

"I do want to have kids. I enjoy the energy and enthusiasm they bring, and I suspect they could teach me as much as I'd teach them. I've been thinking more about it lately." He looked around the quiet cockpit, and she knew they were both thinking the same thing. They'd be lucky to ever get out of here and live long enough to have a child.

"Every now and then I think it might be wonderful to have a baby, to try to give them the happy, warm childhood I've always longed for. But what if I'm even worse than my own parents?" She sighed.

"You'd be a good mother. I can tell."

She laughed, trying to pretend his pointless comment didn't mean anything to her.

"How? You barely know me."

"You're a planner. You plan things and craft them. You'd create a wonderful childhood for them."

"But people aren't like buildings. They have their own spirit and character and might resist every effort of mine to raise them the way I intend."

He laughed now. "So true. I suppose you can only do your best and hope it all works out."

"Too risky for me." She pretended to stretch. Really, she wanted to hide the uncomfortable flash of emotion that roamed through her at the thought that she was too cautious to risk a real family.

"Everything's a risk. You took a flight from Dubai to Bahrain and ended up flying off course into a desert."

"I guess I should have taken that commission to build a family compound outside Dallas."

"It would have been safer."

"But boring. I'd have hated myself for doing it."

"And you'd have missed out on meeting me." His slow smile tripped something inside her. "I won't say I'm glad we're here, but I am glad we're together."

"I hope we're not going to die together."

"I don't think we are." His smile broadened. "I believe I've fixed the radio."

"What?" She leaped forward. Why was he flirting with her when they could be calling for help?

He handed her the headphones, and she tucked them over her ears. "Why can't I hear anything?"

"Listen."

She pricked her ears and heard a low-grade hum of static barely distinguishable from the rattle of the sandstorm outside. "Do we have to be on a particular channel to call for help?"

"I know we need to be on VHF, but I don't know what frequency. There should be a flight manual right here with the information, but the pilot must have removed it. Let's try turning the dial and seeing if we can raise anyone."

They held the headset between them, so close she could almost feel the heat of his breath, and she turned the dial slowly. When they heard a muffled voice, speaking in Arabic, they stared at each other. Zadir cleared his throat, pressed the mic button and spoke into the microphone. "Mayday, Mayday, Mayday."

5

"Mayday, Mayday, Mayday." Zadir's voice rang out again in the tiny cockpit. The speaker on the radio continued the whole time he was talking and didn't stop afterward.

She pressed the earpiece to her ear, hoping for a response. "I don't think he can hear you. What is he saying?"

"It's a prayer."

"We need a prayer. Try again."

He repeated it three times, then she tried, but the man never paused in his recitation of the prayer. Panic tightened her throat. "Do you think the mic is broken?"

"Let's try to find another channel." He fiddled with the dial, repeating the Mayday signal with each turn. Three more times they heard a voice, but it seemed as if no one could hear them. Shoulders hunched together, they tried for over an hour, taking turns to repeat the international plea for help, until they were both hoarse. The ridiculous proximity to Zadir and his intoxicating male aroma would have been enough to drive her mad, but it was even more frustrating to hear people out there, sitting somewhere out there in the civilized world, who could help them out of this nightmarish bind if they could only make contact.

She felt a tear roll down her cheek as they reached the end of the dial for the third time. "No one can hear us."

"We need to rest. There's no sense getting exhausted and wound up. Maybe sleep will give us a fresh idea to try in the morning."

They made their way back into the cabin and drank some water. She offered him some of her food, but neither of them had an appetite. Zadir folded all the chairs in their row down so that there was a flat double bed on either side of the aisle.

"This is very luxurious under the circumstances, but I don't know if I'll be able to sleep."

"Me either." He spread a blanket over the makeshift bed on her side of the aisle. "But we need to take a break and maybe some inspiration will come to us."

"I don't think inspiration will do us much good out here. And the sandstorm is louder than ever." Sand rasped against the windows in gusts.

"We're still alive and in good health and spirits." He stood directly in front of her and placed his hands on her upper arms, which heated the skin there. "This plane was intended to crash without us being aware that the pilot was gone, so we're already ahead of the game. Now we've fixed the radio. Tomorrow we'll have another breakthrough."

"Tomorrow is the wedding. I wonder if anyone's noticed we're not there."

"I guarantee Najib has noticed his best man is AWOL." He stroked her cheek. The gesture made her inhale sharply. "He'll start calling around to see what's happened to me. Eventually they'll find out that our plane never arrived at the airport. As long as the water holds out, we can stay safely here for days."

Her stomach tightened at the prospect of being trapped here for days on end. But it was so much better than the alternative. "What if no one ever finds us?"

"They will. You have to believe that." Now his thumb roamed to her mouth and stroked her lower lip. "We both have a lot of things left to accomplish. You designing my palace, for example."

"And your town. Honestly that's more compelling to me." Why not be truthful? It wasn't likely to happen anyway.

"Why stop at a town? I think it should be a city." He leaned in close enough for her to smell the scent of his skin, masculine and reassuring.

"A whole city? That will take a long time."

"It could be a lifetime's work. You don't think that Baron Haussmann redesigned Paris overnight, do you?"

"I suspect he had a lot of assistants." A smile crept across her mouth in spite of her misgivings. He was far too close to her again, and the way he kept touching her was doing something to her brain. Or to her body. Or both. "I do love the idea of designing a city. One that perfectly fits its environment and makes the most of its natural resources." She was trying to distract herself from looking at his mouth by thinking about design. Solar panels to take advantage of the sun, subterranean aqueducts to irrigate the desert, masonry walls to regulate heat.... It wasn't working. His mouth moved closer to hers, and she felt frozen in place.

Except that she was melting. His lips lowered over hers very slowly, so she could have moved away or stopped him with a hand on his chest or a turn of her head. But she didn't. Their mouths met and her eyes closed as a gust of sensation shook her.

His hand settled on her hip, steadying her, and her fingers rose to touch the bare skin of his back. Warm and supple, his thick muscle soothed and stirred her. He felt so strong and capable, able to land a plane in the wilderness and bring sabotaged equipment back to life. He'd get them out of here, she was sure of it.

His arms closed tighter around her back, pulling her against his hard chest. She kissed him with conviction, wanting to lose herself in this moment of madness and forget where they were and why.

Arousal snapped through her, stronger than she could ever remember, and her fingers slid lower, to explore the waistband of his pants at the base of his spine. Her nipples tightened beneath her thin shirt, crushed against his pecs. She felt his erection thicken against her, and that finally stirred her enough to pull back and stop this runaway freight train.

"This is not a good idea." She blinked. Even the tiny dots of light along the ceiling now seemed too bright.

"I beg to differ." He still held her in his powerful arms, though an inch of steam-heated air now hung between them. "I'm confident we both feel better already."

"We're just losing our minds because of the stress of being stuck here."

"My mind is clear as the Arabian Sea." He looked at her, a smile in his ocean-blue eyes. "And kissing you is the most sensible thing I've done this year."

She almost believed him. He had that kind of charm and charisma. No doubt it had worked on many women before her. "It's late and we're tired."

"Suddenly I'm not tired at all." His teeth flashed in a grin.

She reflected it back. His enthusiasm was infectious. "I can tell." She'd felt his arousal. "But we'd regret it in the morning."

"No we wouldn't." He spoke softly but firmly and laid another kiss across her lips like an offering. Her body hummed with signals telling her to grab this man and hold on tight. Which wasn't her style at all! She hadn't even been on a date in over a year.

She kissed him back, unable to stop her lips from responding. Now his hands roamed to her backside, which he caressed, then to her waist and under her light shirt where they pressed gently into her skin.

A shiver of raw arousal ricocheted up her torso, and she pressed herself against him again. She was hungry for the feel of his skin against hers. She pulled her mouth from his with effort. "I think some primal survival instinct is taking hold of me."

"Me, too. Don't they say you should always trust your gut?"

"I don't think it's my gut that was talking." The area yelling at her was several inches lower and grew hotter and more insistent by the moment. His erection pressed against her, hard as steel. "It's another part that usually gets people into trouble."

He chuckled. "You're not going to believe this, but I have condoms in my bag."

"I believe it." He probably never went anywhere without them, just in case.

He fixed that potent blue gaze on her. "I don't

sleep with every woman I meet, you know."

"Only every other woman?" she quipped.

"Only a woman that I feel a strong connection with. You feel it too, Ronnie. I can tell."

She drew in an unsteady breath. "I feel something, alright. Though I'm not sure what."

He kissed her again. His tongue thrust in to joust with hers and sent a ripple of electricity to her toes. Her hands had somehow snuck into his jeans and cupped his curved backside with gusto. She didn't usually give in to instinct, but right now that seemed the only possibility.

He stroked her cheek. "You're brilliant and beautiful, and for once I'm glad we're trapped here together." He unbuttoned her shirt swiftly—it wasn't even the first time her blouse had been off that day—and touched her breast through her bra. Her nipple tightened and she suppressed a gasp.

"You're handsome and charming and I'm sure I'll regret this, but…" She unbuttoned his jeans and lowered the zipper. With some more tugging and writhing they were both naked on the unfolded luxury seats of the private jet, rolling Zadir's condom on over his impressive erection.

Desire dimmed her doubts and fired her enthusiasm as they wound their naked bodies together, exploring and enjoying each other. He entered her carefully, working his way in gently as she opened up for him and softened in his arms. It felt so wrong—but so good—to let go of her fears, to let herself be swept away by this powerful man.

He guided them in a hypnotic rhythm that made her moan against her will. When she heard the sound of her voice in the sand-swept hush of the cabin, she wondered for a second if she'd totally lost her mind. The answer was simple: of course she had, but there was nothing she could do about that now except surrender to the passion of the moment.

They moved together, sometimes her leading the rhythm and sometimes him. At one point, she climbed on top and brought them both to the very brink of climax, then she slowed the pace and pulled back, prolonging the bliss as long as she could, as if this was the last pleasure they'd have.

Which, given the circumstances, was a distinct possibility. The sudden memory of their grim predicament made her grip him with added force and soon their orgasms propelled them both into an abyss of ecstasy.

Damp with perspiration, panting and shuddering with the aftershocks of their release, they held on tight to each other.

"We probably shouldn't have let ourselves sweat out precious water." Her voice was a raspy whisper.

"I'll lick it back off you." He flashed a cheeky glance from where he lay next to her.

Her belly shook with laughter. Could something that felt so good—and that had released the tension racking her body—really be wrong? She pushed her fingers through his silky hair, feeling affectionate toward this handsome and resourceful man. She didn't want to be anywhere else but in his arms right now.

Though she wouldn't mind being in his arms safe in a comfortable hotel in Bahrain. But if the crash hadn't happened they would have continued the flight without exchanging more than a few pleasantries to each other. He'd never have learned that she was an architect who could design not only his palace but an entire new world for him.

The first misgivings hit her like raindrops falling from a cloud. If she wanted the commission so badly she should never have slept with him. This man was a king, for crying out loud, or soon would be, and he was hardly likely to want a relationship with an American commoner. Their intimacy would be an embarrassment and any attempt at professional relations would be awkward and impossible.

By sleeping with him she'd probably lost out on the commission of a lifetime.

"You're breathing hard." His deep voice tugged her from her thoughts.

"I'm a bit overwhelmed right now."

"Understandable." He stroked her hair, pushing it gently off her forehead. "But I suspect that you'll be able to sleep and everything will seem more doable in the morning. I think the sandstorm is dying down already."

She listened hard and could barely hear the sand flying against the metal skin of the airplane. "That would be a relief. Though I hope it hasn't buried the plane."

"If it has, we'll dig it out. We have plenty of water left, and we'll be good here for a few days. My instincts—the same ones that told me to make love with you—tell me that we'll be rescued tomorrow." He removed the condom in the plane bathroom. They really did have every convenience here. It was kind of funny.

"How?" She wanted to laugh at his confidence, even if it was fake.

"Either we'll raise someone on a radio, or figure

out another way to send a distress call from the plane, or they'll send out a search party and spot us."

"I do hope so." She rested her cheek in the slight depression between his strong shoulder and his thick biceps. It was as comfortable as the finest hotel pillow. He rested his other arm over her, enveloping her in a soothing caress. "I've never had such amazing sex before, and I might want to have it again."

His chest shook with silent laughter. "Clearly, you've been missing out. And I'd be happy to oblige. How come you don't have a boyfriend? I know you're married to your work, but you're very beautiful and must have men following you everywhere."

"I don't think I'm everyone's cup of tea."

"You're certainly mine. I like my tea strong and dark." She felt his smile press against her cheek.

"You might be unusual in that."

"Or I have superior taste. I'm glad no one else snatched you up yet."

She blinked, trying not to take him too seriously. He barely knew her. "I've only had one real boyfriend, and that was in high school."

"How old are you?"

"Twenty-six." She regretted the confession, but she didn't want him to get the wrong idea and think she was someone else.

He stiffened. "So you've been single for…eight years?"

"I've been on dates, but none of them have really led anywhere."

He let out a long exhale of surprise.

"I shouldn't have told you. It's weird, I know."

"Only because you're so gorgeous."

"I did warn you I was married to my work."

"I didn't believe you until now. I'm almost tempted to ask you to get a divorce."

She laughed, but it wasn't entirely genuine. She knew plenty of women, her mother included, who'd abandoned careers they loved the moment a relationship started to make demands on their time and energy. "I'd never give up my work. It's what sustains me."

"I was kidding. Don't take me too seriously."

Now he was letting her down easy. Warning her not to expect anything of him. "Don't worry, I won't." She wanted to bring back the easy calm they'd shared a few moments ago. "And you didn't seduce me into anything I didn't want to do. I enjoyed it."

"Me too." He kissed her cheek. "And now we should get some sleep."

She snuggled against him, trying to keep her breathing slow and steady, like someone who really was about to fall asleep. Not like someone who was about to start sobbing, as she realized—in the esoteric atmosphere of a crashed luxury jet—that from now on the life she'd built so carefully would feel empty and lonely without someone to hold her close.

6

Bright spears of light pounding against Zadir's eyelids announced that morning had come once again to the Rub' Al Khali. He reached out for the lovely woman who'd slept in his arms, but she was gone.

He sat up, rubbing his eyes. "Ronnie?"

"I'm in the cockpit." Her voice stirred excitement in him. Last night had been incredible. Maybe the dangerous situation they were stuck in had unleashed some primordial energy, but he'd made love to her as if their lives depended up on it and the climax had left him too exhausted and drained to even worry about their dilemma.

He sat up and pulled clean underwear and pants from his luggage. Today, he was going to get them both out of there. He took a judicious gulp of water from his water bottle and headed for the cockpit.

She sat in the pilot's chair, looking ridiculously poised and elegant in a crisp, white, fitted dress that set off her gorgeous dark complexion. She turned to him, eyes glowing with excitement. "I found a distress-call button. Or a pull, more accurately. Look." She pointed to a small orange handle far up on the right among the rows and knobs and dials. "I tugged on it right away. I've been doing it every few minutes since."

"Damn, how did I miss that?"

"We were focused on the radio. I think it will send

a signal up to a satellite and let them know we're in trouble. It may even give them our coordinates. You made me think of it last night when you mentioned that there might be another way to send a distress signal."

"You're as brilliant as you are gorgeous." He kissed her cheek and watched a smile spread across her sensual mouth. "Hopefully, now all we have to do is sit here until help shows up. Unless…" An ugly thought had crossed his mind in the dead of night.

"Unless what?" She turned to him, her face so happy and excited that he didn't want to share his fears.

He shoved a hand through his hair. "Unless it also summons the person who's trying to get rid of me."

He watched her smile fade, and she bit her lip with small white teeth. "I didn't think of that. I suppose they thought we'd die in the crash. Now that I sent the signal more than twelve hours later, they'll know that at least one of us survived."

He nodded. "And they may well be the first to get here."

"What can we do?"

"We need to hope that someone legitimate also hears the signal and gets here first. Let's try again to raise someone on the radio."

He donned the headphones and turned the radio dial past the endless recitation of prayers that had brought them no help. A loud burst of static made him start, and a voice in Arabic barked a question: "Is there anyone there?"

It was loud enough to be heard in the cabin, because Ronnie gripped his arm. "What is he saying?"

Foreboding unfurled in his belly. "He's asking if

there's anyone here. You do the talking. Pretend I died in the crash, then if it's the would-be killers they might leave us alone."

She donned the headset, pressed the mic button and started to speak into the mic. "I don't speak Arabic. I've been in a plane crash. I'm all alone in the desert. Please send help immediately."

He watched as a roar of static tightened her muscles. Then he could hear enough to make out a different voice in heavily accented English. "You are alone?"

"Yes, I need help."

The line went dead.

"Can you hear me? I need help?" She looked at Zadir. Then turned off the microphone. "What if they're legit? Do I need to tell them where we are?"

"They can probably tell our coordinates from the distress signal the plane sent out."

"Hello? Are you there?" There was no response. She turned to him, frowning. "This isn't good. Why would they disappear like that?"

"Because they got the information they needed."

"That I'm alone, so they can leave me to die out here?" She held the mic close to her mouth. "Hello, are you sending help?" She shrugged, and even though she'd turned the mic off, she whispered, "I want it to sound legitimate, like I'm waiting for them."

No answer.

"It probably is the bad guys, isn't it?"

He nodded. "But the signal would have gone out to anyone who was listening, so hopefully the Saudi authorities got it, too. I'm assuming we're in Saudi Arabia, because most of the Empty Quarter is within

Saudi borders. They may be trying to contact us on another frequency. I'm sure there's an official frequency for this kind of thing, but I don't know what it is so we'll have to hope we stumble across it."

"Let's keep scrolling. If they could hear you, someone else will be able to hear us, too."

Veronica's tight body was a real temptation but he managed to keep his hands off it while he scrolled up and down the range of frequencies. She was all business today, no flirtation or mention of last night's wonderful lovemaking. He resolved to stay focus on the task at hand.

They'd turned the volume up so loud, using the headset as a crude speakerphone, that even a burst of static fired his adrenaline. Every time they heard the familiar drone of a voice, or even some promising silence, they repeated Mayday and waited with their hearts pounding.

But no one answered.

"It's getting hot in here." Heat pressed against the slanted cockpit windows and poured in through the missing one.

"Soon it'll be hotter in here than outside. We'd better go see if we can reconstruct our circle in case anyone is looking for us. The plane is probably covered in sand."

He followed Ronnie out of the cockpit, trying not to let the lilt of her slim hips hypnotize him as she swayed across the tilted plane. He probably shouldn't be thinking about her gorgeous body at a time when they needed to work fast to save their own lives, but it was hard not to.

It took some effort to get the plane door open, as sand had piled against it during the night. Naturally all their hard work of yesterday had been obliterated. "You go rest and drink some water. I'll drag a circle in the sand." He wanted to be a hero, to save both of then and whisk her off into an air-conditioned sunset. Every hour they spent out here brought them closer to the end of their water. Even if they paced themselves, their supply would last a day or two more, at most.

She jumped down to the sand. "There's no way I could sit idle right now. Two of us will get it done faster."

A sense of urgency fired adrenaline through Zadir's muscles. He was sure that he was the reason they'd been stranded there and left for dead, and he had no intention of letting his enemy win.

7

Stunned, Sam kept waiting for the garland to reach "What was that?" Tiny hairs stood up on the back of Ronnie's neck. The air seemed to grow hotter and more oppressive as they stood outside the plane, wondering how to make it more visible now it was coated with a thick layer of dust. They'd cleaned off the call numbers and the windows. Now the atmosphere around them suddenly seemed to throb.

"A helicopter." Zadir spun around. "I can hear it but not see it."

"Oh, my gosh," her nerves jangled. "We have to make them spot us!"

"I wish we had a flare, but whoever sent us here removed them. We'll have to wave something. Grab an item of clothing."

She pulled up a pair of pale ivory pants they'd laid as part of their circle, and he grabbed a white shirt. They started to jump up and down, waving the items over their heads.

Still no sign of a helicopter. Gasping already in the intense heat, she paused for breath. "Has it gone past us?"

"I can still hear it." He frowned. "I think it's circling around us. It must be hidden by the high dunes."

"Do you think it could be the person who disabled the plane?"

She watched him inhale deeply. "Could be. But they may also be our only way out."

"Not if they shoot us on sight. You need to hide inside the plane."

"I'm not hiding. I'd rather die in the open."

Her instincts recoiled against that fate for him, or for her. "Not me. I'd rather live to bring them to justice."

He scanned the horizon to the south. "I see them. It's a dark helicopter. I don't see any markings."

"What do rescue helicopters look like?"

"The Saudi ones are mostly white, with red stripes."

She peered at the shape growing larger in the distance, rotors thumping. "That's not white." Fear clutched at her chest. "Get inside, Zadir. I mean it. If it's the bad guys, they can take me back to civilization and I'll send help for you." She couldn't bear the thought of seeing him get shot, or worse.

He glowered for a moment. "I don't want to put you in unnecessary danger. I'll lay low at least until we can figure out what's going on."

"Get in the shade under the wing." She watched as he crouched in the dark recess. If necessary, she'd use her wits to get them both out of there.

Instead of growing closer, the helicopter continued to circle around the crash site. Frustration gathered inside her. "What the heck? Why aren't they coming in to land?"

"They're trying to figure out what's going on here. I think you were right to have me hide. They want to be sure you're alone."

"Then they'll leave. They'll know I won't survive out here." The prospect chilled her, even in the burning heat of the morning sun.

The throbbing of the rotors echoed the pounding of her heart. Someone out there wanted Zadir dead and didn't care if she lived or died. Anger flashed through her and she wanted to yell at the dark copter, but she managed to keep her head, and her tongue.

"There's another helicopter." Zadir's low voice rumbled out from beneath the wing. "I can't see it from down here but I can hear it. Scan the horizon."

She spun and instantly saw a pale helicopter approaching from the North, the opposite direction of the other. "It's white. With a red tail."

"Those are the good guys."

Without a second's hesitation she jumped on the wing, glad of her shoes on the burning metal, and started to jump up and down, waving the ivory pants. "Help! Help me!!" Unlike the dark helicopter, the white one changed course and headed straight for them. "Help! We need help!"

She scanned the horizon for the dark copter and saw it disappearing off to the south again. "The first one is leaving."

"They don't want to be seen near the scene of the crime," Zadir said grimly.

"Come on out. They're heading right for us."

Zadir jumped up on the wing next to her as the helicopter approached, circled the site and landed about fifty feet from the plane, kicking up a sandstorm to rival last night's and making them clutch their impromptu flags to their faces to keep the dust out of their eyes and nose.

Men in overalls came running across the sand, calling out in Arabic. Zadir responded, and the men helped them down from the wing. She was tempted to go jump directly onto their waiting helicopter, but Zadir reminded her she might want her computer and phone, if not her clothes, so once their vital signs were checked and they'd drunk some water, they retrieved their possessions from the plane and boarded the helicopter.

The propeller was so loud that it drowned out all noise in the Spartan interior. She could probably have told Zadir she loved him and wanted to bear his children, and he wouldn't have heard her. Since they were both in good shape, the medics agreed to take them to a base in Dammam, near Bahrain, so they could drive to their destination.

"I'm not sure I'll ever get on a plane again," she admitted, as they climbed down onto blissfully hard tarmac.

"Then you'll have to live your life in this part of the world." Zadir grinned. "Designing my palace and city."

"That might be an excellent idea."

They freshened up at the hospital, then kissed all the way to Bahrain in the back of the taxi.

"We'll be there in time to dress for the wedding. It's at sunset," she murmured, when they came up for air.

"And we'll have to tell and retell the story of how we survived a plane crash in the desert."

"Or we could keep it as our little secret." She didn't really want anyone to know she'd been rash enough to get naked with Zadir while their lives hung in the balance. And the whole ordeal was so emotionally and physically exhausting that talking about it seemed an overwhelming prospect.

"That's probably a good idea, since there's someone out there who wants me dead. I suppose it's bound to get out into the media that a small plane crashed."

"No one needs to know that we were on it, though, do they?"

"I suppose not. I'll have to tell my brothers so we can start searching for the culprit. But we'll tell them the full story together when you come with me to Ubar and meet them." His deep blue gaze and warm smile made her heart swell with joy.

"The full story?"

"Maybe we'll keep some of it just between ourselves." Zadir lowered his lips to hers and kissed her, softly at first, then harder, until she didn't know right from wrong, up from down or the desert from the deep blue sea.

THE END

Read more about Veronica, Zadir and his brothers, and find out who's behind the attempts on their lives, in the rest of the *Desert Kings* stories.

Desert Kings Short: Veronica – Stranded with the Sheikh
Desert Kings: Book 1: Osman: Rescued by the Sheikh
Desert Kings: Book 2: Zadir: Bought for the Sheikh
Desert Kings Short: Mistletoe Butterfly
Desert Kings: Book 3: Gibran: Return of the Rebel Sheikh
Desert Kings: Book 4: Amahd: Captivated by the Sheikh

Be the first to know about Jennifer Lewis's new releases! Sign up for her newsletter at www.jenlewis.com

Read on for an excerpt from **Desert Kings: Osman: Rescued by the Sheikh**.

1

"We're going to die out here." Allan punched more numbers into his dying phone, his sandy hair blowing in the desert wind.

Samantha took one more peek under the propped hood at the nonfunctioning engine of their Land Rover. "We'll be fine. We'll just hunker down until morning. Then someone will come along the road and we'll get help." She shivered. A menacing chill had descended over the desert as the sun sank below the distant horizon. "We should build a fire to keep warm."

"And to keep animals away. There are probably jackals and hyena out here." Allan glanced nervously around. "But there's no wood."

Scraggly trees poked here and there out of the arid scrub, she saw no loose branches. Probably the local villagers gathered them as soon as they fell. "We could run the engine for the same effect. But it won't be long before we run out of gas. This thing's a guzzler." Sam tapped the Land Rover's dusty white exterior. Something in the distance caught her attention. Specks of light, moving toward them.

"There's a car coming."

"What?" Allan jumped. She could barely see him

in the thick dusk. Sam became increasingly aware of the natural smells around them and the tiny movements of invisible creatures.

"I'll turn the lights on so they can see us."

"No! Don't." Allan hurried toward her. "What if they're bandits? These empty stretches of desert are full of outlaws."

His chicken heartedness annoyed her. "Maybe they'll give us a ride back to civilization."

"Or take us prisoner and send ransom demands to our families. I knew we should never have taken on this project. Who cares about a wedding festival in the middle of nowhere, for crying out loud?"

"It's never been filmed." She shivered again. "We're capturing a moment in history." The lights grew steadily closer, possibly illuminating the way for nomadic warlords armed with semiautomatic weapons. Goosebumps pricked her arms.

"There may be a good reason film crews never come here." Allan's teeth chattered.

She stroked his back. "Just relax. Let me do the talking." She'd had romantic visions of them joining in the celebrations at Nabattur, celebrating their love under the stars. Instead, their love was being tested by setbacks that threatened to derail the whole project. Their flight to the airport in Medina had been delayed, so they'd missed their connecting flight and had to take a tiny puddle jumper on a journey almost longer than its gas tank could handle. They'd now driven for six hours, and dreams of hot showers and cool hotel sheets were evaporating in the dry desert air.

The quiet purr of the approaching engine suggested a large sedan rather than a paramilitary vehicle, but all she could see was the blaze of white headlights. Heart pounding, she turned on their hazard lights and started to wave her arms. All they needed was a ride into Nabattur. Or maybe just someone with a flashlight and a little mechanical expertise. Despite a flicker of apprehension, she gritted her teeth and crossed her fingers as the approaching car slowed to a stop on the loose surface of the dirt road.

The blinding headlights hid their potential savior—or kidnapper—from view as the car door opened. She squinted as a large, unmistakably male silhouette materialized dressed in the long robe favored by the locals. A gruff voice addressed them in Arabic, with an expression she didn't recognize.

She attempted, in halting Arabic, to explain that they'd broken down. She could hear Allan's labored breathing behind her. The man swept around their Land Rover and looked—in the dark—at the silent engine.

"You'd better come with me."

It took her a moment to register that he'd spoken in English. His low voice sounded kinder in the less guttural tongue. She wished she could see his face.

"Could you take us to Nabattur?" She cursed her voice for shaking.

"You can stay overnight in my home. It's just a few miles up the road. In the morning, we'll find a mechanic to retrieve your vehicle."

"Oh." She turned to Allan. This was the kind of warm desert hospitality she'd been told to expect. Was it too good to be true? "What do you think, sweetie?"

She heard him swallow. "I think we should stay

with the car."

Frustration filled Sam's chest. This man was trying to help them and now Allan wanted to insult him by refusing his offer of hospitality. She turned to the stranger. "I don't want to be a bother, but are you able to call a tow service for us? We can't seem to get any cell service here."

His throaty laugh rang out in the empty desert. "A tow truck? At night? Do you think you're in New York City?" He gestured to his car. "Grab your bags and jump in. I wouldn't leave anything behind. There are some unsavory characters on this road at night." His voice dropped for the last sentence and made her wonder if he included himself in that group.

They had two choices. They could stay here and face whoever else might wander along the road that night. Or they could go with someone whose intentions and motivations were unclear, but who at least spoke English. Right now the latter seemed like an easy choice.

"Let's get our stuff." She jostled Allan gently to push him into action, and before she had time to talk herself out of it, they were piling their duffel bags of clothing and equipment into the back of his black Mercedes.

Their rescuer ushered her into the front seat next to him and Allan into the backseat behind her. She realized, as she buckled her seat belt, that she hadn't introduced herself. In fact, she hadn't even looked at him properly yet. The interior lights were still on from the doors opening, and she turned sideways in time to catch a bold profile with a strong, aquiline nose and a determined chin. His head was bare and his hair cropped quite short. He turned to look at her, and she felt the full force of his dark gaze for a split second before the lights went out.

She recognized him instantly. Those eyes shone with fierce intensity from even in the grainiest newspaper photo, and she'd seen several during her research. In fact, she'd had a hard time getting his strongly hewn features out of her mind. She thrust out her hand, determined to keep her head. "I'm Sam Bechtel. Samantha."

He took her hand but didn't shake it. Instead, he held it for a moment, as her palm heated against his. "Osman Al Kilanjar, at your service."

She resolved not to be intimidated, even now that she knew for sure that their rescuer was a member of the ruling family. And was taller and more handsome in person than she'd imagined from seeing his photos. His English was excellent, with a hint of a British accent, which wasn't exactly surprising since she'd read that he was educated overseas.

Not exactly the armed bandit Allan had anticipated. She started to relax a bit.

Then he lifted her hand to his mouth and kissed it.

An odd sensation, powerful and unsettling, flashed through her, and on instinct she jerked her hand back. He let go, and it slammed against her chest. Her heart pounded, and her just-kissed hand throbbed with awareness.

She felt as if he'd just claimed her.

"I'm Allan Strano," came a thin voice from the backseat. "We're here in the desert to shoot a documentary about the festival. Our car broke down a couple of hours ago and yours is the first car we've seen."

Her heart swelled to hear her fiancé galloping to

the rescue. Likely the hand kiss was just some archaic custom of the region and she was reading too much into it. She sucked in a breath and tucked a loose strand of hair behind her ear. "I'm the producer, and Allan's the director. It's so frustrating to break down when the festival starts tomorrow. We need to be in Nabattur to record the opening ceremony."

"When the streets are strewn with rose petals." His voice was very deep, with a hint of humor. She saw his eyes gleam in the dark.

"Yes, thousands of rose petals. It seems extraordinary to sacrifice so many flowers in a place where it must be so hard to grow them."

His low chuckle filled the car. "Perhaps the roses are the lucky ones, to participate in such a joyous occasion. You know it's a festival of love?"

"Yes. A group wedding ceremony. I did as much reading as I could about it." Which wasn't much. This region was both obscure and impenetrable due to geographical isolation behind several intimidating ranges of mountains. Which only made her more excited to explore it for herself.

"We take love seriously here in the high country. Most of our songs and stories address it. Our world is harsh and demanding, and the choice of your life's partner is the most crucial test." His low voice crept into her ear.

"A test? I've never heard it described that way before." Allan piped up from the back seat.

"Absolutely." He fixed his gaze on her, which was disconcerting, even in the dark. "Choosing the wrong partner brings the worst kind of bad luck. Some believe that our ancestors will come back to haunt us if we make a poor choice."

"I suppose it's all about picking someone who can be fruitful and multiply," muttered Sam. Traditional cultures sometimes set her teeth on edge. At least this region didn't seem to believe in more barbaric rituals like clitoridectomy.

"Of course." She saw the glimmer of white teeth. "Continuing the family line is of paramount importance."

"What about companionship?" she protested.

"Essential." He held her gaze just long enough for her to become self-conscious about her breathing. This man made her very uncomfortable. A kinder person would try to put two stranded strangers at their ease, not stare at them until their pulse rate doubled while lecturing them about choosing their mate.

She wondered if he knew Allan was her boyfriend. Fiancé really, but she didn't wear a ring because they were both concerned about avoiding blood diamonds and hadn't decided what to get. In fact, Allan had never actually proposed to her, but they'd discussed marriage and decided to go for it, so since then she'd considered them officially engaged.

A glance at the speedometer alarmed her. The car was doing nearly seventy on this desert lane in pitch darkness. Osman Al Kilanjar must know the road well, as little of it was visible even with the high beams on. The desert stretched out all around them, dark and empty. She knew the ever-present mountains were out there, too, shrouded in blackness. "How far away do you live?"

"Far enough."

"How long will it take to get there?"

"Not long."

The shine of his teeth irritated her. She wondered what kind of house Osman Al Kilanjar lived in. Simple two-room houses of mud brick where the usual type of local dwelling, but some more nomadic types still lived in large and elaborate tents that housed an entire extended family on the move. He seemed like the tent type, but if he was the future king....

His hand gripped the wheel as he swerved at high speed. She gasped and clutched the dashboard.

"Hey!" called Allan. "What are you doing?"

"My apologies. I just avoided a collision with a gazelle." His stern profile betrayed no sign of amusement, to her relief. She watched his hand slide slowly back into position. Broad across the knuckles, with long, strong fingers, they were powerful, intimidating, even. Mr. Al Kilanjar exuded masculinity from every pore and she could smell it, even over the strong scent of the leather upholstery.

Or maybe it was sweat. Possibly her own. It had been more than twenty-four hours since they left New York.

"Allan, did you bring the phone chargers?"

"Oh, shit." She heard the sound of him slapping his forehead. "I left them in the car. I wanted to charge the phones while we were driving."

"It's my fault." She could feel her phone in her pocket. Barely charged and useless as a lump of desert rock until they could find some coverage. "I meant to put them back in my bag."

"I did lock the car, so hopefully no one will steal them."

She glanced at their captor. Wait, he was their rescuer, so why did that word spring to mind? He didn't seem at all interested in their conversation. Likely he couldn't care less if their whole car got stolen.

"Almost there." He took a sharp turn to the left, into further impenetrable darkness, and drove along at frightening speed toward distant points of light that pierced the blackness.

"Is that a town?"

"In a manner of speaking."

"You talk very formally." She said it as lightly as possible.

"The result of my very formal education."

"Cambridge?" she guessed. She hadn't researched the royal family since they weren't directly relevant to her project.

"You're not entirely wrong. I attended Oxford as an undergraduate, but my business degree is from Harvard, which of course is in Cambridge, Massachusetts."

She saw a smile tug at his mouth.

"Cute." She smiled back. Oxford and Harvard were reassuring. He certainly wasn't dumb or crazy if he'd gained entry to both of those. "I'm a hippie from UC Berkeley, I'm afraid."

He chuckled. The sound was surprisingly pleasant.

"Allan's a film geek from NYU." She didn't want Allan to think she'd forgotten all about him. "And we both live in New York."

The flickering lights in the distance grew brighter until she could see they were flaming torches mounted on a high stone wall with an arched opening. They drove through the arch into a well-lit oasis where palm trees lined the road.

"Welcome to my home."

Wow. The stone ramparts seemed even taller from the inside, illuminated by more blazing torches. To complete the medieval setting, long-robed men darted out of the shadows and opened his door, then their doors as well. Mosaics of colored marble decorated the walls, and brass incense burners added luxurious fragrance to the air. Their host spoke rapidly, and his men's impassive expressions gave no hint of what they thought about having visitors.

Her heart leaped when she saw them pulling her and Allan's bags from the trunk, but a brief protest was ignored and their bags were carted off through a tall pair of wood doors.

"Uh, that's my equipment." On instinct she followed her bags. The camera alone was worth nearly thirty thousand dollars. Leaving her host, she followed the traditionally garbed men down a stone-floored hallway. Round arches leading into other rooms lined the space. She glanced back to make sure Allan was following. "Sweetie, we need to keep an eye on our bags," she hissed.

"I know." His face looked grim. He realized they were way out of their depth.

"Don't worry. We won't steal your treasures." Osman Al Kilanjar's voice boomed out behind Allan. This was the first English he'd spoken since they arrived. He'd addressed the men in a confusing local dialect that she couldn't follow.

"I didn't mean to imply that you would." She swallowed.

"Your caution is well placed." He strode toward her, coming up behind Allan. He was a good head taller than Allan, who seemed to shrink in his presence. "You are among strangers. Perhaps our customs include extracting payment for our hospitality from our guests' possessions."

"I did a lot of reading about Ubar in preparation for my trip, and several texts mentioned the legendary hospitality of the region." She attempted a smile.

A wolfish grin spread across their host's wide mouth. "All your needs will be taken care of. Perhaps even those you did not yet anticipate."

She frowned and looked ahead. They'd reached the end of the hallway and another high arched doorway. One of the men in the striped robes rapped on it with his knuckles, and a small, high grating opened. This must be some kind of inner sanctum.

The door opened slowly to reveal a beautiful woman in a turquoise silk dress. The woman's eyes dropped to the floor at the sight of Osman, and she shrank back to let them pass.

She, Samantha Bechtel, might be his guest here overnight, but she had no intention of showing such humiliating deference. And she kept a sharp eye on their baggage as the men carried it along another hallway lined with doors under pointed arches.

This place was huge, and she was pretty sure she recognized it from her research. "Is this the fortress of Al Kaur?" She turned to Osman, defying him to ignore her question or give an enigmatic non-answer.

"It is. First erected around four thousand years ago to defend my ancestors from the marauding efforts of the neighboring Azrib tribe. Rebuilt and expanded many times since. For the last four hundred years or so it has been the seat of the ruling family of Ubar."

She hadn't yet revealed that she knew who he was. Perhaps it was better to pretend surprise. "So you're royalty?"

“Indeed I am. “He looked infuriatingly smug.

As well he might if he was to be king.

Then again, who’d want to be king of this desolate stretch of rock-strewn desert?

He’d caught up and now his stride matched hers. Then he leaned in to whisper in her ear. “And perhaps one day you will be too.”

2

"I have met my wife." Osman let his words sink in as he watched his brothers stunned faces. They sat on low cushions around the enormous traditional hookah the servants kept preparing despite his continued insistence that none of them smoked. Their father had smoked a bowl of something or other every day, and apparently he was expected to continue the tradition. The air was thick enough already. Incense smoldered in a brazier in one corner, and beeswax candles burned in several hanging lanterns, casting flickering light over the multicolored mosaics on the walls.

Zadir spoke first. "You'd marry an American?"

"Why not?" Osman had ushered Samantha to their finest guest chamber, where she was changing for dinner. He let his mind briefly stray to wonder what she was wearing right now. "I've spent most of my adult life in the U.S. Most of the women I've dated are American. Why would you find that strange?"

"That was when you lived in America." His younger and more serious brother Amahd gestured with his hands. "It's one thing to date a girl in the land of milk and honey, quite another to bring her back to this barren wilderness and ask her to live here."

"I'd hardly call our ancestral homeland a barren wilderness." They'd all grown too used to Western luxury. "Besides, we can maintain a residence or two abroad."

"You can hardly be king and live somewhere else."

"I'm sure I wouldn't be the first."

Zadir ran a hand through his already tousled hair. "I think we've found the real reason our father decided to split the throne between the three of us. He wasn't sure which—if any—of us he could count on to come back and stay."

Osman frowned. He'd secretly dreaded his father's death, not out of filial devotion but because of the responsibilities that came with his passing. As the oldest son he'd long been expected to ascend the ancient throne of Ubar in the tradition of his ancestors. It had been a slap in the face when he discovered that his father had rewritten the Monarchic Accord to divide their nation into three equal-sized principalities, promising one to each of his brothers as well.

He had half a mind to wash his hands of Ubar and its problems and head back to New York. Then something more primitive—stupidity, probably—tugged at his heart and made him determined to ascend the basalt throne of his ancestors.

"Our father may have had a heart of stone, but he was a very intelligent man. I think he knew that if he got the three of us here together we'd figure out a way to see this thing through."

Amahd frowned. "Perhaps he intended for us to prevent each other from making rash mistakes like marrying a foreigner."

Osman glared at his brother. "Don't be such a stick in the mud. Besides, Ubarite tradition tells us that we will feel the call of destiny when we see our intended mate."

Amahd shook his head. "You've barely met her."

Zadir smiled. "It sounds like our brother has fallen victim to love at first sight. What's her name again?"

"Samantha." He tested the word on his tongue. He liked it. Substantial and a little hard to handle, just like its owner. Seducing her promised to be a fun challenge. "She's making a documentary about the festival, so she must be interested in our culture."

"That sounds promising enough to me." Zadir raised his coffee cup.

"You've both lost your minds." Amahd inhaled deeply. "Choosing a bride is a great responsibility, especially when we need to set an example for everyone in the country. There are many beautiful Ubarite women who'd love to be queen."

"Tell me about it." Osman raised a brow. "I'm tired of gold diggers throwing themselves at me. If anything, Samantha has done the opposite so far. In fact she's been rather rude."

"Maybe she's rude because she knows you're a king. Americans hate monarchs."

"Yes." He'd enjoyed the stunned look in her eyes when he'd suggested that she might join the ruling family.

She hadn't bothered to reply. No doubt she assumed he was joking. Maybe he was teasing her at that moment, but already the prospect of pursuing her had seeded itself in his heart.

Since the news about his father's death four months ago had made the rounds, women were practically climbing up to the palace windows on ladders trying to get an audience with him. It was not likely these crown-seeking ladies were the kind of partner and soul mate he craved yet seemed unable to find.

"I think she's cute." Zadir, a connoisseur of women himself, grinned. "I saw her arrive."

"What about that guy she's with?" Amahd was always more cautious. Trying to figure out the angles before jumping in.

"What about him?" Osman stretched his arms and shoulders. "She works with him. If anything, his presence here will give her the confidence to relax in our midst."

"He's her boyfriend." Amahd poured himself a tiny cup of coffee from the tall brass urn.

"No, he isn't." Osman frowned. "A woman like Samantha would never be interested in such a… wimp."

Zadir chuckled. "Whether she is or not, they're together. I saw her kiss him when they went into their rooms."

"What?" Indignation flashed through him. If he didn't know better, he'd almost think it was jealousy. But since he'd barely even met her, that was impossible. "If they're a couple, why didn't they ask to stay together?"

"Perhaps they're aware that unmarried couples shouldn't cohabitate in our culture," said Amahd. "And she just doesn't want any trouble."

Osman stood and paced across the dimly lit space. Samantha and that feeble excuse for a man? On the other hand, American women did have some strange criteria for choosing their mates. Someone had told him that they considered a sense of humor to be the most important characteristic in a man.

A sense of humor? That wouldn't get you too far in the heat of battle.

Or in bed.

"If I need to liberate Samantha from an unfortunate union with the wrong man, then so be it. Fortune smiles on the bold."

Desert Kings: Osman: Rescued by the Sheikh is available now.

ABOUT THE AUTHOR

Jennifer Lewis loves heat in all its forms including spicy food, steamy temperatures and smoking hot heroes. She is a USA TODAY bestselling author and her books have been translated into more than twenty languages. She lives in sunny South Florida and when she's not sitting at her laptop she can often be found at the beach. Read more about her books and join her new release mailing list at www.jenlewis.com.

Printed in Great Britain
by Amazon

10317448R00041